P9-BZG-949

Disney

FROZEN

BABYSITTING THE TROLL TOTS

Disney PRESS
Los Angeles • New York

Written by Brittany Rubiano
Illustrated by the Disney Storybook Art Team

For information address Disney Press, 1101 Flower Street, Glendale, California 91201.
ISBN 978-1-4847-4769-8
F383-2370-2-15195
Printed in China
First Edition, September 2015
1 3 5 7 9 10 8 6 4 2
For more Disney Press fun, visit www.disneybooks.com

Anna pulled on her boots. Her friends Kristoff and Sven would be there any minute. It was a beautiful spring evening, and they were going to watch over the troll toddlers while the adults went to their annual magical prophesying convention.

"Are you sure you don't need me to come?" Elsa asked. "I can provide some magical help."

"I think we've got it covered," Anna said, giving her sister a quick hug. "They're just babies. How hard could it be?"

Soon Anna, Kristoff, and Sven set off. As they rode to the trolls' valley, Kristoff told Anna stories about growing up with the sweet and silly creatures.

"I wonder if I should have brought games," Anna said. "Do trolls like games?"

“Oh, don’t worry,” Kristoff responded. “They’ll probably sleep the whole time. I bet we’ll be relaxing by the fire. Maybe eating some snacks.”

He explained that Bulda, his adoptive mother, set a very strict bedtime for all the young trolls. Sven grunted in agreement.

As Anna, Kristoff, and Sven entered the valley, dozens of mossy rocks rolled toward them. Suddenly, the trolls appeared, and a chorus of greetings erupted.

"Kristoff! Sven! Anna! Welcome! We missed you!" the trolls called out.

Bulda looked Kristoff over. “It seems like just yesterday you were young enough to have a sitter,” she said.

“Remember when all he wanted to do was run naked through the valley?” Grand Pabbie asked.

“Oh, really?” Anna asked, stifling a giggle. “You never mentioned that.”

“Okay, that’s enough stories for now,” Kristoff said.

Bulda led Anna and Kristoff to the troll tots. “If they get hungry, you can feed them smashed berries. And they may need a leaf change. But it’s just about their bedtime, so they should be sleeping soon.”

As the adult trolls headed off, Anna waved. “Have a great time! Everything is going to be . . .”

"A DISASTER!" she finished.

The toddler trolls had escaped from their pen when no one was looking. Now they were running, climbing, and swinging all over the place.

"Oh . . . no, no," Anna said, rushing to help a few trolls who were climbing up a boulder. "That's dangerous."

Kristoff ran to a leaning tower of trolls that had sprouted.

"All right, guys," Kristoff said, gently pulling the trolls off one another. "Let's settle down now."

But the more Kristoff, Anna, and Sven tried to calm the little trolls, the wilder they became.

“Maybe they’re hungry!” Anna said, heading for the basket of smashed berries.

“Yummy!” she cooed, offering one of the toddlers a spoonful of berries. But the trolls clearly felt they had better things to do.

"Maybe they need changing," Kristoff said. He bravely peered into one of the trolls' nappy leaves. "Nope."

"Let's put them to bed," Anna suggested. "They must be tired by now."

But alas, the young trolls were wide awake.

Suddenly, a cheery voice interrupted them.
“Hello, troll babies!”
It was their friend Olaf!

"Elsa sent me in case you needed some help," Olaf explained, turning to the trolls. "Why, hi there. Ha-ha! That tickles!"

"Boy, are we glad to see you," Kristoff said.

Anna ran to greet the snowman. But in her hurry, she tripped and fell face-first into the basket of berries!

"Whoaaa!"

Kristoff rushed to her side. "Anna! Are you okay?"

Anna lifted her head. Her face was covered in dripping purple goop.

The little trolls burst into loud giggles. They stampeded toward her and lapped up the berry juice on her cheeks.

Anna laughed. "Well, I guess that's one way to feed them."

After the trolls were done, they sat in a heap, happy and full. Suddenly, a strange smell floated through the air. The trolls looked down at their leaves.

"Uh-oh," Kristoff said knowingly. "Olaf, you distract them."

Olaf told the little trolls a story while Anna and Sven collected leaves and Kristoff changed diapers. Soon everyone was clean and sweet-smelling once more.

"And now for a showstopping song!" Olaf announced.

Anna noticed that the trolls were swaying. Some of them were having trouble keeping their eyes open.

"Actually," she said, "maybe Kristoff and Sven would like to sing a lullaby instead."

"Good thing I brought my lute," Kristoff replied, while Anna and Olaf began putting the trolls to bed.

"Rock-a-bye troll-ys, in your small pen," Kristoff sang.

"Time to go sleepy for Uncle Sven," Kristoff as Sven crooned.

By the time the adult trolls returned, the toddlers were sound asleep.

"Wow, great job," Bulda whispered.

"It was easy," Anna replied, elbowing Kristoff.

"Piece of mud pie," Kristoff added.

Bulda smiled and hugged her friends. "You two will be great parents someday!"